KING DAVE
ROYALTY FOR BEGINNERS

OXFORD
UNIVERSITY PRESS

Great Clarendon Street, Oxford OX2 6DP

Oxford University Press is a department of the University of Oxford.
It furthers the University's objective of excellence in research, scholarship, and
education by publishing worldwide. Oxford is a registered trade mark of Oxford
University Press in the UK and in certain other countries

British Library Cataloguing in Publication Data

Data available

ISBN: 978-0-19-276399-0

1 3 5 7 9 10 8 6 4 2

Printed in Great Britain

Paper used in the production of this book is a natural,
recyclable product made from wood grown in sustainable forests.
The manufacturing process conforms to the environmental
regulations of the country of origin.

KING DAVE
ROYALTY FOR BEGINNERS

FROM THE
MOST BONKERS MIND OF

OXFORD
UNIVERSITY PRESS

STAY BACK,
ALBRECHT!

CHAPTER 1

Once there was a dragon, a dragon called Dave.
Dave wasn't a normal dragon. He was the King's
official hero consultant, brave knight, amateur
wizard, and was known throughout the kingdom
for his excellent carrot cake. But Dave would
not be famous for these incredible deeds at all,
without his trusty steed and best friend, Albrecht
by his side.

When they were together, there was nothing to fear . . .

Albrecht was all about action and being very loud.

Dave had a way with words and preferred to talk things over.

'Why is some Dummkopf message man running into me when I am trying to be casually cool?!' said Albrecht as he brushed himself down and examined his scraped knees. 'Dave! Did you see this? Dave? Where is Dave?'

Having given the troll very clear directions, Dave ran over to Albrecht. 'It was just a mistake, Albrecht, and to be fair it does seem very urgent.'

The messenger uncrossed his eyes, leapt up and starting shouting, 'THIS IS URGENT! VERY URGENT!'

'OK, I understand it's urgent, but maybe you need to just calm down? Would a nice cup of tea and some carrot cake help?' said Dave.

'No, no, no, this is part of the service,' said the messenger. 'This message has been sent as a Most Very Super Urgent message, the most urgent type of post we offer. It's a premium service and the running, shouting, and arm waving is included as part of the package. On top of that it's from the actual King himself! Oh, and it's for you. See for yourself.'

The messenger thrust the scroll into Dave's hand and resumed the running and shouting.

Dave did his best to tune out the noise and started to read.

Dear Dave,

This is the King himself and this is a Most Very Super Urgent Message! I had to pay extra to make it this urgent, but I did rather like the idea of all the shouting and running around. Now, it's very important that you come to the castle RIGHT NOW! Like I said, it's pretty urgent.

Lots of love,
The King

P.S. Tell Albrecht I said hi.

Dave and Albrecht looked at each other.

'Mein Gott,' said Albrecht, 'something terrible must be happening; the King would never pay extra otherwise. Maybe he is being kidnapped, or someone's put a curse on Princess Rubella again, or the castle is on fire!'

'Or have you made him angry again by arm wrestling the other knights?' said Dave. 'Either way, I think we have to go right away!'

How much
did you pack?

CHAPTER 2

Dave and Albrecht sprinted all the way to the castle, which wasn't easy with legs as short as Dave's. On their approach to the castle steps though, Dave and Albrecht started to wonder if all that exercise had really been necessary.

The King and Princess Rubella were waiting for them, surrounded by suitcases. Nothing was on fire and they both seemed absolutely fine.

'Finally, there you are!' said the King. 'Our taxi is already here.'

'Dad, we really have to go. We'll miss the welcome drinks,' called Rubella from the coach.

Dave and Albrecht panted their way to the top of the steps. Albrecht grabbed for the King and said, 'Your tiny Majesty! Is everything okay? Are you on fire?!'

'Obviously not,' said the King.

'We're here to help!' said Dave. 'Whatever the emergency, we can handle it.'

'Oh, I wouldn't have said it's an emergency,' said the King.

Albrecht scowled. 'But we RAN. All the way.'

'It is very urgent though chaps.'

'Why is it urgent?' Dave asked.

'Because we're going to miss the WELCOME DRINKS!' shouted Rubella from the coach again.

'Yes, I know!' said the King. 'We're in a bit of a tight spot, Dave my boy. You see, we're going to the 111th Annual Kings and Queens Conference. We can't possibly miss it because the keynote speaker is Queen Belinda of Potatoland! I'm such huge fan, I thought I might even ask her to marry me . . . but anyway! She'll be talking about Managing Your Peasants, Hugs Not Hitting. Very exciting.

'We really need someone to keep an eye on the kingdom while we're away. It's only for a week.'

'Dad, WE ARE LATE!' shouted Rubella.

'I KNOW!' The King turned back to Dave with a pleading look on his face. 'I'd asked Boil Man to take care of things, but when I told Rubella, she said that was the stupidest decision a king had ever made, which I thought was a bit mean.'

'But ACCURATE!' shouted Rubella.

The King looked slightly hurt but continued. 'So, we both agreed that Dave, as official hero consultant, knight, and all round good chap, would be the perfect choice to kingdom-sit instead. How about it?'

'Oh yes, I'd love to!' said Dave. 'But Albrecht and I are a team so . . .'

'A team led by Albrecht!' said Albrecht.

'Um yes, if you like,' said Dave. 'We are a team, so I think we should run the kingdom together.'

'Oh no! You couldn't possibly do that,' said the King. 'Only one person can rule. One crown, one king. That's how it works.'

'Fine by me,' said Albrecht. 'I couldn't possibly be King of Castletown anyway, because I am already King of the Seagulls and it would be a conflict of interest.'

'What?' said the King.

'Don't ask, it's a very long story,' Dave said. 'Albrecht, will you be my special advisor, and chief best friend of the King?'

'It would be my pleasure. I am very good at

advice and friendship,' Albrecht said.

'Dad, I am going to leave without you!' Rubella slammed the coach door.

'OK Dave! Ideally I'd like to do a proper induction about being king, but as you can see time is in short supply.' The King opened up his suitcase and pulled out a sword.

'Sorry, this is just my travel sword, not the huge shiny official one, but it'll have to do. Dave, I hereby crown you temporary King of the kingdom.' He tapped Dave on the shoulders with the sword.

'Oh, and you'll want to read this. It'll tell you everything you need to know about being king.' The King pulled a book out of his suitcase.

Royalty for Beginners! I know you like a good book Dave, and this old chestnut is the best one on kinging. I've included lots of my own notes, so it's particularly excellent.'

'Oh super,' said Dave. 'Just a couple of questions before you go. What day should I put the bins out? Do you have a first aid kit just in case? Where is the . . .'

'DAD! I AM LEAVING WITHOUT YOU!'

Rubella snapped the coach window shut and it started to move away.

'No time, Dave!' said the King running for the coach. 'Just make sure you look royal. Wear a crown! You're not the king without a crown! You'll find spares in my wardrobe.'

The King leapt onto the coach and it galloped off towards the conference.

'Well,' said Albrecht, 'there goes our weekend plans.'

Dave looked at Albrecht. 'Being king is a big job. I'm not sure I know where to start or even if a crown would suit me! I'm worried all the gold will clash with my green complexion or that I'll accidentally start a war or . . .'

'Worry not, Dave,' said Albrecht. 'We'll just do as the book says and you'll be an über king. Let's go and try on some outfits.'

Royalty
for BEGINNERS

CROWNS

The most important thing a King can have

The one who wears the crown rules the Kingdom.

Lose the crown, lose the Kingdom.

Standard

For everyday use.

Tiara

Looks excellent
With ballgowns.

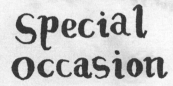

Special
Occasion

Only for official
state occasions
and Christmas.

CHAPTER 3

After a bit of rummaging in the King's wardrobe,
Dave was looking thoroughly royal.

'How do I look?' asked Dave.

Albrecht eyed him with raised eyebrows. 'Sehr gut, but I'm surprised you didn't pick this über crown here. Maybe it would look sehr gut on my own head . . .' Albrecht lifted a particularly huge crown off its velvet cushion and gave it an experimental prod.

Dave looked horrified. He dived for Albrecht and took the crown out of his hooves.

'No, no, no, Albrecht! You can't touch that. It's the Special Occasion Crown and the book made it

very clear that it's strictly for special occasions.'
Dave gently placed the crown it back on its
cushion. 'And besides, you can't wear a crown if
you're not technically King of Castletown.'

'Yes, I suppose I should only ever wear my
King of the Seagulls crown. Did I ever show it to
you, Dave? It is very impressive and also makes
for an excellent snack.'

Yes it is entirely made of chips because of all things seagulls value chips the highest.

'Oh, how . . . greasy,' said Dave. 'Now that I
look all regal I should probably get on with some
royal duties. I really want to do a good job and
impress the King and Rubella. There's a useful-
looking chart here in the book about what I
should be doing.'

A king or queen has certain duties they must perform.

DUTIES

INSPECT THE KNIGHTS

DO THE PAPERWORK

DRESS FANCY

WAVING

OPEN THINGS

ATTEND PARTIES

KEEP PEASANTS CLEAN

WIN WARS

OH, ALSO TAKE CARE OF THE KINGDOM

'It's not what I expected,' said Dave, doubtfully.

'Meine Dave,' said Albrecht, 'it's time to get waving.'

So Dave set about his royal duties.

He inspected the knights.

Albrecht, do you think I'm doing this right?

Just look serious and nod and you'll look very royal.

He did lots of waving at people.

28

He got all the paperwork done.

And he even found something to open. 'Oh gosh, which big scissors should I use? There's so much to learn,' said Dave.

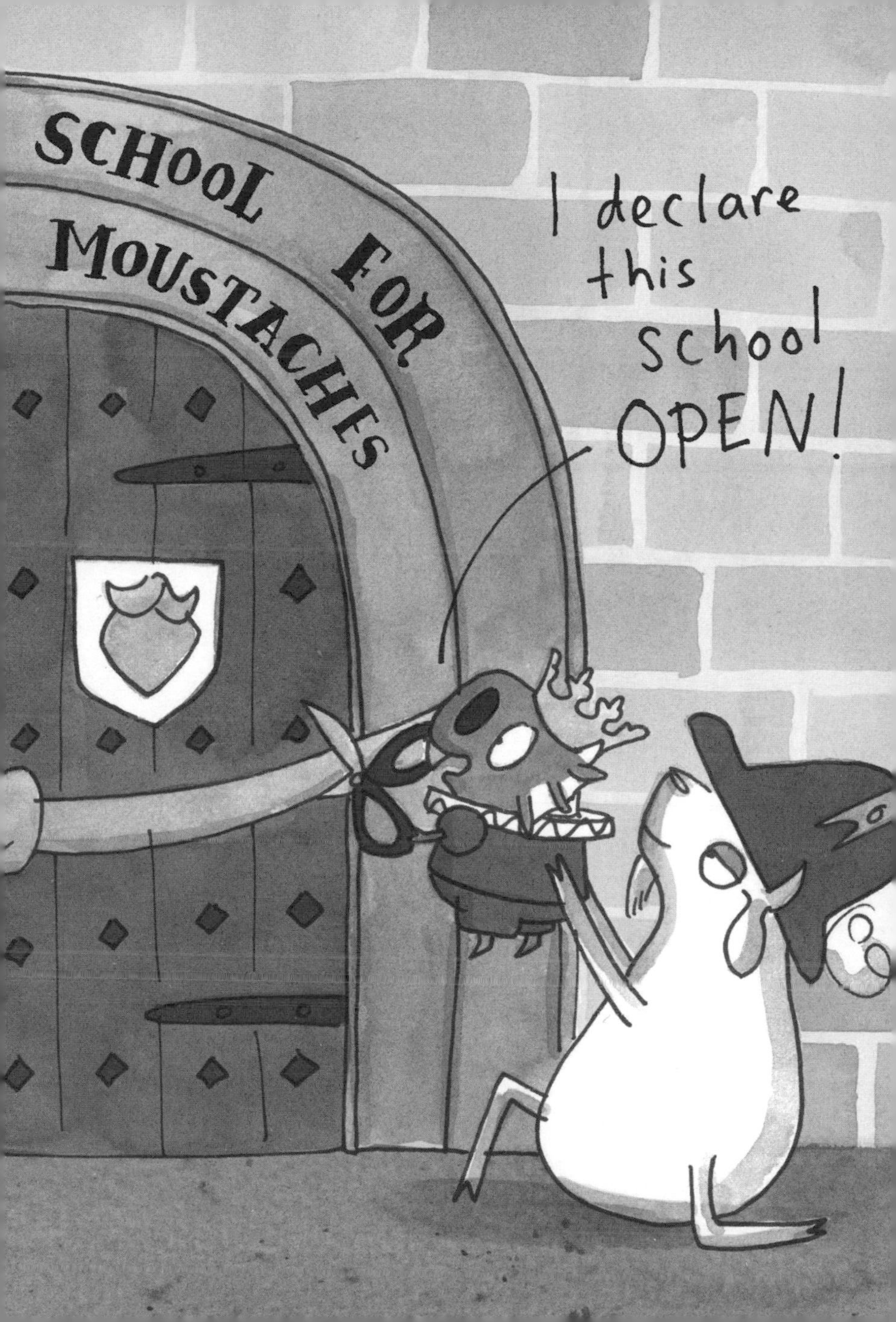
SCHOOL FOR MOUSTACHES
I declare this school OPEN!

Dave felt as though he was getting on top of the royal duties, but there were some things about being king that Dave found a little odd. A guy with a trumpet started following him around and playing a fanfare whenever he entered a room. The staff kept putting caviar on all his food even when he just wanted a cheese sandwich for lunch. And whenever he said hello to anyone, they would bow really low and back away slowly.

After a very long day of things being weird, Dave had an even stranger experience when it was time to go to bed.

35

Dave sat in bed with his cocoa feeling a little shocked. He felt a lot shocked when out of nowhere Albrecht popped up from under the covers.

'Guten Abend, Dave!'

'Wahh!' said Dave. 'Where did you come from?'

'I've been in this bed the whole time. Those men scrubbed your teeth good, ja? This bed is so super huge you could hide a comfy army in here. But Dave, I have news! I was in the kitchens not looking for night-time snacks when I saw the calendar on the wall. There is a big note on it in red pen saying that the ambassadors are coming to visit tomorrow!'

'Oh, my gosh!' said Dave. 'Hang on, what's an ambassador?'

'They're very important guests from other kingdoms. Mein Dave, it is very important you impress them so they go back and tell their kings and queens how this kingdom is super amazing.'

'Right! Oh my, the King must have forgotten to tell me about this before he left. If I'm going to be a good king I need to find a way of impressing these ambassadors. I must look at the book and make a plan. I think I'll invite them to my book club; that's very impressive.'

'No Dave, book club is an excellent good time but not impressive. You must throw them the most super awesome party that they have ever seen. Do not worry though, I have planned parties so wild that people are still cleaning up the mess. Albrecht will take care of this.'

'That's very nice of you, Albrecht, but I really think I should take care of this by myself. If I'm going to be a responsible king I need to take care of my own royal duties, and that includes party planning. I'll need to organize some decorations and lots of fun games. Oh, party hats! They're a must.'

'Huh, if you are sure Dave, but I should tell you I am the original party animal. I think I may have been the first animal to ever throw a party.'

'I'm sure I can do this, but now we should get a good night's sleep. Have some of this cocoa and we'll have nice dreams about super parties.'

Dave snuggled down into his acres of covers, tired from his bustling day. He'd got on top of all his royal duties, picked out an outfit, and had quite a complex bedtime. Being king had turned out to feel very strange so far. But planning a party was OK; he could definitely do that. What could possibly go wrong?

Ambassadors

These are royal employees that come to visit from far away kingdoms. They then report back to their king or queen about you and your kingdom.

Know your Ambassadors

KINGDOM of SOMEWHERE

GUILD of WIZARDS

UNICORN KINGDOM

MERMAID KINGDOM

TROLL TOWN

POTATO LAND

You must impress all the ambassadors so that they don't think you have a rubbish kingdom and that you're a rubbish royal.

41

CHAPTER 4

Dave and Albrecht watched from a distance as ambassadors from all the nearby kingdoms started to arrive.

'There are so many!' said Dave, leaning so far over the battlements he nearly lost his crown. 'Look, I can see the Troll ambassador, the Unicorn ambassador, the ambassador of Somewhere, the Mermaid ambassador, the ambassador of Potatoland with her potato hat and, hey, look! There's the ambassador from the Guild of Wizards, Magical Mark! How exciting. I'm sure they're going to love it here.'

'Ja, I have not seen such a menagerie of party guests since I played pass the parcel with six hamsters, a peacock, and a shark,' said Albrecht. 'I won the prize and the shark ate me. Speaking of eventful parties, have you got yours all set up and ready, Dave? We must make sure those ambassadors are über impressed.'

'Oh yes, I spent all morning making food and blowing up balloons. Don't worry Albrecht; I consulted *Royalty for Beginners*, and I've got a pretty amazing party all ready. I think they'll all be very impressed.'

Party!

The king must be the life and soul of the party.

There must be music. Get your best minstrels in.

Good food is a must. Roasted things are always a hit. Try roast boar, roast peacock, roast a whole giraffe if you have a big enough castle.

Lay on some entertainment. Nobles will always enjoy jousts, archery, and hitting peasants.

CHAPTER 5

Dave's party was a disaster. No matter how many party games he suggested or homemade sausage rolls he gave out, the ambassadors looked seriously bored.

Sausage roll?

Albrecht walked over to Dave and removed his party hat. 'Dave, as your friend it is my duty to always be honest with you. This party is the most rubbish party in the whole history of parties. If we do not do something soon all the ambassadors will go home and tell their royals that we are super boring rubbish people and that you are the most boring of us all. This is not good.'

Dave set down his tray of uneaten sausage rolls. 'Oh wow, OK, that was very honest, Albrecht. We can't have that news reaching Rubella and the King! OK, how can I get this party started?'

'We shall use my party planning skills. I shall make this the most memorable party since I escaped from inside that shark and then got everyone to do the hokey pokey!'

'Amazing! Thank you, Albrecht! You're the best friend and life coach that a dragon could ask for,' said Dave.

'Yes I have won many awards for my fabulous friendship.'

'You shall be in charge of snacks. You're the King so the kitchens should make whatever you ask for. Go and ask for some exciting snacks. On no account should there be any sausage rolls. We'll meet back here in an hour; I have got some favours to call in.'

CHAPTER 6

It was then that Dave realized everyone was
staring at him.

'Um, is everything OK?' said Dave.

'Oh my good gracious!' said the butler. 'Your Majesty! This is very unexpected. Noble, wise, and well-dressed kings never come down here to the lowly kitchens full of humble servants and recycling bins. I never thought I'd see the day.'

'Oh, sorry Mr Butler,' said Dave. 'Am I not supposed to be down here?'

The butler looked horrified and threw himself to his knees. 'NO! Forgive me please, Your Majesty! Of course a wonderful and well-spoken king like yourself may go anywhere he wishes. Isn't that right everyone?'

All the chefs dropped to their knees too with a chorus of, 'Yes, Your Majesty! Of course, Your Majesty! I like your shoes, Your Majesty! Would you like some pie, Your Majesty?'

Dave was a little taken aback but not unhappy. 'Oh my, that's very nice of you. You're all so helpful. Yes, they are nice shoes aren't they? OK, hang on; I'll just make a short speech.'

Dave clambered up onto a stool and cleared this throat. 'Hello very helpful staff. I have come down to the kitchen as your majestic and noble

King to see if you had some snacks I could bring to my party. I was thinking maybe some dips would be nice. It wasn't going very well, you see, and Albrecht thinks . . .'

The butler leapt up. 'Snacks! Of course, Your Majesty will have snacks! We have the best snacks. Chefs! Show his majesty what we've got.'

Finger sandwiches!

Squirrel parfait!

Chicken! Chicken! Loads of chicken!

Quadruple decker ice cream!

The chefs burst into action, snatching up dishes and parading them past Dave.

Dutifully Dave began to sample all the snack food.

Dave sighed. 'I don't know how I can decide.'

'Oh, don't worry,' came a voice from near the fire. 'They just love this nonsense. All the parading and groveling and bum kissing. They thrive on it.'

A black cat unfurled itself from a basket next to the fire and started rubbing itself against Dave's legs.

'Ooo hello nice kitty.' Dave gave the kitty a stroke.

'Oh, I'm no kitty; I'm Miranda. You've probably heard of me. I'm such a fabulous being that even kings will stroke me.'

'You can talk!'

'Yes, I have indeed been cursed with the talking spell like your smelly goat friend, but it does mean that everyone can enjoy my scintillating conversation. You must be the temporary king then? I can tell because of your silly hat and all the fuss those ridiculous chefs are making.'

'I rather like the crown; it's a good fit and all nice and shiny. Hi, I'm Dave. I'm just taking care of things until Rubella and the King get back.'

'Kings. There's always such a fuss about kings.

I just don't understand it. They're just people, often with short tempers and terrible dress sense.' Miranda made side eyes at Dave.

Hey! I chose this outfit myself!

'Plus they're rarely even cats and they're certainly never me, so why would anyone even care?' Miranda sank her claws into Dave's legs for no good reason.

'Ouch?! You have a very high opinion of yourself don't you?'

Miranda absent-mindedly swatted her paw at the legs of one of the parading chefs. 'Of course I do, I'm a cat. It's kind of our thing. And you have no idea how I struggle. It's very hard being so excellent, but the absurd butler expects me to run about all day eating mice like a common servant! What I wouldn't give for some cream.'

'Oh, I'm sure we can find you some cream amongst all this food. Excuse me? Mr Chef? Do we have any cream?'

A chef carrying a tray of ice creams flung them to the floor, rushed over to the table, and ran back to Dave with a huge bowl of cream. 'Would Sir like some caviar on that?'

'Ew no,' said Dave. 'Miranda, you can have this cream as long as you promise to be more polite to people, please?'

'Yeah, whatever,' said Miranda.

Dave gave her the cream and was a little relieved that it stopped her from talking.

'Oh my, I still have to choose some snacks,' said Dave, looking at the chef parade that had now taken over the entire kitchen.

'Why bother?' said Miranda looking up from her cream. 'You're the King; they'll be thrilled to give you all that snack food and more, the idiots. Just say you'll take it all and make them stop this ridiculous parade. I can't bear all the racket while I'm eating.'

'That's not a very nice way of putting it, but I see your point. Gosh, I did waste a lot of time making sausage rolls this morning when I could have got these very helpful chefs to do it all for me! Excuse me, Chefs? All your snacks look delicious, so do you think you could please take them up to the great hall?'

All the chefs stopped their parade, looked at Dave and gave out a cheer. 'Three cheers for the excellent King Dave! He is the best at choosing snacks! Dave is wise and glorious! May he have all the dips his heart desires!'

The chefs who weren't carrying trays lifted Dave up onto their shoulders and paraded him back out of the door.

'I am the best at choosing snacks,' thought Dave, feeling a little pleased with himself. 'To the party everyone!'

LiMBo!

SNACKS FOR ALL!

CHAPTER 7

The all-new, restyled and rebooted party was a huge success. Albrecht had pulled out all the stops. He called in favours from his time in the music business, and got Lightning Steve and his electric minstrel band to do the music. He had barrels of his favourite drink, Supermint

Mouthwash, sent in. He'd turned the lights down low, lit scented candles, brought in puppies for people to play with, set up a limbo pole, and Dave hadn't done a bad job with the snacks either.

'See, I am still the original party animal! Are you pleased, Dave? Didn't I do a fantastic job?' said Albrecht. 'Aren't I, Dave? Dave? Where is Dave?'

Albrecht couldn't see his friend anywhere, so he went to look for him. Albrecht crossed the dance floor, slipped under the limbo pole, grabbed a Rat-On-A-Stick from a passing chef, and then spotted Dave by the mouthwash. He was having a lovely chat with the ambassadors. They seemed to be getting on really well now . . . Wait a minute! What was Dave saying?

Albrecht listened as Dave addressed the ambassadors.

' . . .and then I went to my kitchens. Yes! Me a king in the kitchens, crazy I know.

Well, I had the staff bring up the snacks and then the party was AMAZING! It was easy really.'

Albrecht couldn't believe what he was hearing!

He stormed over to Dave. Anyone can order snacks, but it was Albrecht who had made this party awesome.

'Dave! What are you doing?!' shouted Albrecht.

'That's King Dave,' said the ambassador of Potatoland.

'Fine!' said Albrecht and shouted louder, 'King Dave! What are you doing?'

'Albrecht, you're interrupting my conversation! This is very important diplomacy.' Dave grabbed another ice cream cone from the dining table and ushered Albrecht into a corner.

'Dave, you know I turned this party from super rubbish to über amazing! You can't just say it was all you. I called in all my best favours and let them use my professional grade limbo pole.' Albrecht folded his armed and pouted. 'This is not like you, Dave.'

Dave started to feel a bit guilty, but there were more important things than Albrecht's pride at stake here. 'Look Albrecht, it's very important to make sure they think I'm a good king, but this is an excellent party and you deserve a reward for all your hard work. I'll give you a reward like a king would. Albrecht, please kneel.'

'I am not going to give you a piggyback now, Dave.'

'No Albrecht, that's not what I mean. Just kneel.'

Albrecht looked unconvinced, but he got down on one knee anyway. Raising his ice cream into the air Dave said, 'Albrecht, I declare you Lord High Albrecht of All The Things!'

Dave tapped Albrecht on the shoulders with his ice cream. 'Kings reward their subjects with fancy titles, so I've given you one like a real nobleman, or noblegoat. Mr Butler? Will you go and get Lord Albrecht a fancy uniform?'

Albrecht seemed to have forgotten all about the party. 'Lord of All The Things, eh? Can I have some medals?'

'Sure,' said Dave.

'Excellent,' said Albrecht.

The next day Albrecht came down to breakfast in his new uniform. He had polished all the shiny buttons and was looking forward to seeing what Dave had planned for the day. But when he caught sight of Dave in the great hall, Albrecht felt his good mood draining away.

'Albrecht!' called Dave from across the hall. 'Look! The ambassadors enjoyed the party so much they didn't want to leave! Isn't that great?

The Potatoland ambassador suggested they stay an extra night and maybe have another party. That was some really fabulous kinging, even if I say so myself.'

Dave turned his attention back to the ambassadors. Albrecht was perturbed. He

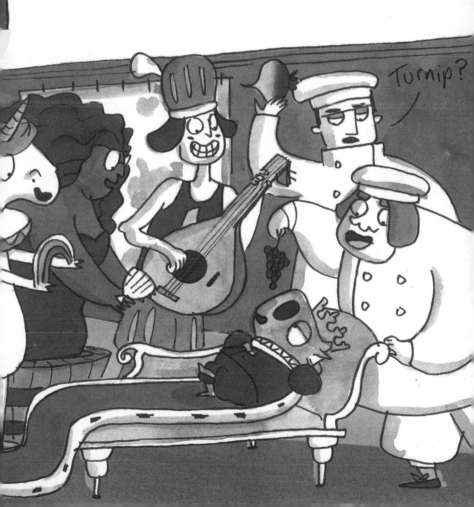

thought that he very much suited being Lord of All The Things, but all the fancy medals in the kingdom couldn't stop him from noticing that something was different about Dave.

CHAPTER 8

Later that day, Albrecht was looking out of one of the castle windows when he saw Dave striding around the grounds with his pack of ambassadors following him closely. He noticed that the one from Potatoland seemed to be laughing particularly loudly at Dave's jokes.

'This does not seem very like Dave,' Albrecht said to himself. 'Wah . . . OW!'

Albrecht looked down to see Miranda, who had just scratched him.

'Why did you do that, cat lady?!'

'Oh, no reason,' said Miranda, 'but I couldn't help overhearing you, and yes, you're right about Dave. I've seen a lot of dubious kings during my time here as the most fabulous cat in the castle, but this does not look good for Dave. Follow me.'

Miranda slunk off down the corridor and Albrecht, intrigued by this mean cat, did as he was told and followed behind her.

Miranda led Albrecht to the King's office.

Look. He hasn't touched the paperwork.

'Sometimes we all get behind with the paperwork, ja?' said Albrecht doubtfully. 'I have not done a tax return for twenty-six years.'

'If that was all I had to show you, you tax-avoiding goat, it wouldn't be so bad, but I'm not done,' said Miranda.

She led Albrecht into the royal bedchamber and pointed through the door where Dave was now doing something very un-Dave-like.

Looking good!

'Mein Gott! What is this, Dave?'

'It's just a little portrait, Albrecht. The ambassadors said I should get one done; it's just what people expect of a king.'

Albrecht stared, wide eyed, at the giant portrait. 'Dave, I've lived in houses smaller than that portrait.'

The artist leaned around the canvas. 'Could Your Majesty stop moving or I shall mess up your noble nose?'

Dave straightened up. 'I'll talk to you later, Albrecht. We wouldn't want him to ruin my noble nose.'

Too perturbed to look at Dave's noble nose any more, Albrecht returned to where Miranda was scratching up a tapestry while she waited for Albrecht to return.

'It's always a bad sign when they start getting portraits painted,' she said. 'There's something else you should see in the great hall.'

'We keep these metal-coated fools around the castle so they can guard it from invaders, stand around looking shiny, and occasionally joust for my entertainment. If they're too full of leftover sausage rolls to move, then that's no good at all,' said Miranda as she sat on a sleeping knight's head. 'A good king should keep them on a short leash, like people should do with those awful things they call dogs.'

Albrecht gave one of the sleeping knights an experimental prod, but he didn't move. 'It isn't like Dave to let people nap on tables when they should be helping. This isn't the kind of behaviour I expect from him.'

'But this is the sort of behaviour you generally get from kings. Trust me I've seen it all. There's one last stop on our castle tour that I want you to see.'

Miranda led them up several flights of spiral stairs up onto the top floor of the castle until Albrecht was sweating and puffing.

'This better be worth the exercise, cat lady,' said Albrecht.

Miranda leapt up onto Albrecht's shoulder and wrapped her tail round his head. 'Oh, yes it is. Have a look at this.'

Miranda pointed towards a doorway through which Albrecht could see a long corridor covered in paintings. 'This is the castle portrait gallery. It shows every ridiculous king or queen this kingdom has ever had and what they did wrong.'

'Look, here are the ones who didn't do their paperwork.

'And here are the ones that didn't keep control of their knights.

'And, well, here are the ones which spent too much time having paintings done of their noble noses, which is why we have this gallery in the first place.

'But the point is they were not very good kings or queens. I remember them all vividly, interrupting my sleep with their invasions or being loud when they met their grisly ends.'

'If you remember all these kings and queens, how old are you really, meine Katze?' said Albrecht.

'A feline never reveals her age!' Miranda swiped a paw at Albrecht's face. 'Look, the current king is only alright because he's got people like Rubella and myself to tell him when he's being an idiot and doing stupid things like trying to put Boil Man in charge of the kingdom. You need to keep your king on the straight and narrow too. Go and have a serious talk with Dave before his actions make my home all loud and messy and he ends up with his portrait on this wall.'

Albrecht took Miranda's advice and went to find Dave. He found him in the King's wardrobe where he came face-to-face with something even more scandalous than the nose painting.

CHAPTER 9

'Dave! Is that the Special Occasion Crown you're wearing? What is the occasion?!'

'Oh no, nothing special,' said Dave. 'I thought with me being King and everything it would be a shame not to wear the best crown. Otherwise it'll get all dusty won't it?'

'But Dave, the Special Occasion Crown can't just be worn on a normal Wednesday! You said yourself that it is only for the most special of days. You've been so busy trying on crowns and getting your portraits done of your nose that you haven't done any kingly duties, and the knights have eaten so much party leftovers they say they have tummy ache too bad to move. They're not doing their jobs.'

Dave continued looking at the crown in the mirror. 'You could argue that every day is special when you're a king. And plus, the ambassador of Potatoland says it looks very fetching on me and that I should definitely get distracted by looking at it in the mirror all day.'

'But the kingdom, Dave! Stop thinking just about crowns. I am starting to think those ambassadors are a bad influence. I cannot wait for them to leave.'

'The Potatoland ambassador said you would say that because you don't understand that the King knows best and doesn't need to be given good advice all the time.' Dave stepped forward to look Albrecht in the eye but when he moved the oversized crown gave a wobble and slid right down over Dave's face with a thunk.

'Murph murph morphmurhp mioph!' said Dave, muffled from inside the crown.

Albrecht gave a snigger. 'I cannot hear you, Your Majesty. Are you stuck in your big fancy crown?'

'MURPH!' said Dave.

Albrecht rolled his eyes, walked over to Dave and took hold of the crown. He gave it a hard yank and it popped off, sending Dave rolling across the floor.

'Sehr regal, meinem King,' said Albrecht.

Dave let out a furious gasp and scowled at Albrecht. 'Look Albrecht, now my outfit is ruined! I've got another ambassador party to attend this evening. The Potatoland ambassador said everyone was having such a good time that they should stay on a few more days.'

'They're staying?!' said Albrecht.

'Yes, they're staying! You see, it's going really well, so I just don't have time to deal with those stupid knights and all those other things . . . I know! As the King I hereby declare Wednesday, Thursday, and Friday to be the knights' days off. That'll give them time to get over their tummy ache.'

'But Dave, that means the castle will be vulnerable to attack until the weekend and you know how the peasants get rowdy on a Friday night,' said Albrecht.

'That might be so, but how could the knights

possibly defend a castle with tummy ache? Stop worrying and help me find another crown. Then come outside and see what I've built.'

It's a pool party!

CHAPTER 10

'It's a pool party! The Mermaid ambassador just insisted we have one,' said Dave.

Albrecht dipped a hoof in the water and shuddered. 'Dave, usually I love the pool parties especially if you have the snorkels. It reminds me of my time in the underwater city of Atlantis when I was MerAlbrecht.'

'But this pool party I cannot approve of. Surely this has used all the water from the well? What will we drink?'

'Oh, you do worry too much, Albrecht,' said Dave. 'I've already thought about that. I've asked the chefs to put in an extra large order of lemonade. It should be here by Friday, and plus everyone likes lemonade better than water, right guys?'

'Oh yes,' said the Unicorn ambassador. 'I only drink fizzy. Still is so common.'

'A king should only be seen drinking soft drinks, and there's no need for a convenient water supply,' said the ambassador from Potatoland.

'Oh yes, you're so right, King Dave. Canonball!' said Magical Mark the wizard ambassador as she dived into the pool, splashing water all over Albrecht.

Dave tittered and the ambassadors started to laugh too.

'Look at your goat friend!' giggled the Potatoland ambassador. 'He's far too damp for us to take his good advice seriously!'

Albrecht gritted his teeth. 'Dave! I thought we were friends. I won't stand here and be made a fool of.'

'You got to admit, Albrecht, it was rather funny,' said Dave.

Albrecht stormed out of the courtyard. 'What sort of Dave would laugh at people and hurt their feelings like that?' thought Albrecht. Not that Albrecht's feelings were hurt because he's far too brave and magnificent for hurt feelings; but if they were, Albrecht would have had just about enough of King Dave and his bad attitude.

That night, Albrecht went to bed angry. In the morning, still feeling furious, he went to the royal tennis courts to work off some aggression. Luckily, his tennis partner, Mildred the Bearded Lady, was there. As Castletown's resident doctor and educator of girls with moustaches, Albrecht had always found her a good person to talk over his problems with.

'Do you really think Dave is doing such a bad job of being king? He really helped out at the opening of my new school.' said Mildred, as she hit the ball back with a furious forehand.

'That was at the beginning of the week and now things have changed. He wears the special crown, which is only meant for special occasions, gets big Dummkopf paintings done of his nose,

and builds swimming pools for no good reason!'
Albrecht returned the ball with a lacklustre
backhand.

'It's always hard starting a new job. You've got
to expect Dave to make a few mistakes.' Mildred
smashed the ball over the net and Albrecht
barely bothered to hit it back. 'Match point!
Albrecht, you're really not on your game. This is
not what I expect from a previous winner of the
Castletown Open.'

Albrecht chucked his racket at the umpire.

Mildred picked up Albrecht's racket. 'I think you just need to sit down and talk things over with him. Why don't you give him one last chance? Come on, let's go and get a drink in The Dragon's Head and we can go and find Dave afterwards.'

Albrecht and Mildred stepped out of the Castle Sports Centre and were confronted by what could only be described as big trouble.

Albrecht started to back away from the angry peasants. 'Mein Gott, this is more than one goat can handle, even a most spectacular goat as I!'

'It is a pickle,' said Mildred. 'I should go back to the school and make sure my girls are alright.

'This is a job for a king!' said Albrecht. 'Not even new Dummkopf King Dave will be able to ignore this problem.'

Peasants. Yes, no one likes them, but as a royal it is your responsibility to take care of them and make sure they're happy. Mistreating your peasants can lead to riots, outbreaks of plague, bad smells and having chickens thrown at you. Fortunately, there's three easy things you can do:

1

Keep them clean. Regular watering is recommended.

2

Share the love. Give them lots of hugs.

3

Let them know you care. Listen to their problems.

Ignore your peasants at your own risk!

CHAPTER 11

Albrecht managed to assemble the peasants in the throne room.

So, the peasants explained to Albrecht what the problem was.

I am the maker of Original-Rat-On-A-Stick, Castletown's favourite snack.

Then I came along with All-New-Rat-On-A-Stick* and everyone loves it!

NEW RAT-ON-A-STICK

It doesn't even contain real rat!

SO?

* contains no real rat.

STOP! I'll get the King.

Albrecht looked everywhere for Dave. He wasn't in the swimming pool; he wasn't in the great hall eating snacks, or lost under the piles of paperwork.

On his way out of the royal office, Albrecht spotted Miranda by the door, eating All New Rat-On-A-Stick.

'Snooty Katze! Do you know where Dave is?' said Albrecht, urgently.

Miranda looked up from her meal. 'I can't believe there's no real rat in this! How slimming. Oh, it's you, smelly goat man. Yes, I saw him with the ambassadors in the Royal Library.'

'I smell of nothing but the finest goat! Rude mouse eater, do you know what they're doing in there?'

'Well, greasy grass eater, they seem to be planning something, but I'm too excellent to care about their silly plans. You need to sort that Dave out.' Miranda started purring around Albrecht's hooves.

'I'm trying! I suppose I must see what Dave is up to myself if you're too busy to help, cat face.'

'I don't care,' said Miranda.

'I like trading the insults with you, cat lady; we must get coffee some time but now I must find my friend.'

'Fine. I like cream in mine.'

The library entrance was unguarded (Thursday is the knights' day off now) so Albrecht shoved open the doors and trotted in.

Albrecht strode up to the table. 'Dave, your subjects need you. You see, there is Rat-On-A-Stick, but now there is also All New Rat-On-A-Stick . . .'

'That's *King* Dave, Albrecht. We mustn't forget protocol,' said the ambassador for Potatoland.

Dave hopped down from his throne and sidled over. 'Albrecht, as King I'm obviously far too busy and important to deal with the problems of lowly peasants. Can you imagine it, a king talking to peasants!'

Dave looked at his ambassadors and they all started giggling.

Albrecht was definitely not giggling. 'The Dave I know would love to talk to peasants and solve their problems. What could be more important than that?!'

'I'm glad you asked, Albrecht. Something brilliant we've been working on for the kingdom. My friends, the ambassadors, assure me that this is just what the kingdom needs. Look at this!'

Dave clicked his fingers and one of the ambassadors held up a poster.

'It'll be an amazing celebration of all things Dave,' said the Mermaid Ambassador. 'And it's going to be tomorrow and there'll be a launch party tonight! Won't that be fun?'

'It's what every royal should have,' said the

Troll ambassador. 'An excellent idea from the Potatoland ambassador!'

'Yes, it'll be a brilliant distraction,' said the Potatoland ambassador.

Albrecht's eyes bulged. He'd never thought he'd see Dave act like this. No more second chances. 'I have never seen anything so vain and self-centered, and I've met Miranda!' Albrecht couldn't stop himself leaping on the table and stamping his hooves. Dave Day posters scattered everywhere. 'You're not acting like a king; you're acting like a Dummkopf.'

The ambassadors gasped.

'I'd never speak to my King like that, not for all the rainbows in the kingdom!' said the Unicorn ambassador.

'Trolls respect their royals. What kind of a kingdom is this?' said the Troll ambassador.

'You should banish that insolent goat who talks perfect sense,' said the ambassador of Potatoland.

Dave hesitated. He looked at Albrecht and then looked at the ambassadors and then looked back to Albrecht and then back to the ambassadors again.

'Mien Gott, Dave, what kind of king can't even make a decision?!' shouted Albrecht. 'I cannot bear this faffing, so I declare myself banished just so I don't have to be around you Dummköpfe anymore!'

Albrecht turned round about to storm out.

'You can't banish yourself!' Dave called after him. 'Only kings can banish people, so I hereby declare you banished anyway!'

Albrecht slammed the door behind him.

Dave turned back to his ambassadors. 'Well, I think I handled that one well.'

They all nodded.

CHAPTER 12

The National Dave Day launch party was already in full swing.

Get your Dave Day merch!

CUDDLY DAVE

FLAGS

T-SHIRT

Ever since Albrecht's argument with Dave, he had noticed a sicky feeling in the bottom of his stomach. Yes, Dave was acting über crazy, but maybe if he hadn't shouted Dave would have listened to him. He thought he'd try and talk to him one more time. As Mildred would say, it's always better to try and sort things out.

Albrecht had been truly shocked when he tried to get back into the castle and realized that he really was banished. He just didn't think Dave would go through with it. Well, if that's the way Dave wanted it then Albrecht would not talk to him again. And if this was what best friends were like these days, then Albrecht decided he would be better off sitting on the battlements on his own and drinking all the mouthwash he could find.

Once Albrecht got up on the castle walls and looked across the land away from Castletown, he saw something that definitely shouldn't have been there.

Stupid Dave doesn't protect his kingdom...

Thinks he's so fancy...

...bad friend ... banish <u>ME</u>?!...

CHAPTER 13

Alone, Albrecht had been trotting through the night to find the source of the lights.

Finally he reached the edge of the forest. He peered out of the branches.

A Potatoland army! I know an army when I see one, and this one is ready to attack, thought Albrecht. Not only that, but Albrecht recognized this queen from the conference poster the King and Rubella had. Queen Belinda of Potatoland! She wasn't at the conference; she was here, planning to invade the kingdom while Dave was distracted. And there's the Potatoland ambassador! Albrecht knew she was a bad influence, telling Dave to throw all those parties. What a devious plan and who even needs so many crisps?

Albrecht couldn't let the kingdom fall. If only Dave wasn't so busy playing at being King, he would be here with Albrecht and he would have a simple plan and clever words to sort this whole thing out. Albrecht was well aware that simple plans and nice words were not his forte: big entrances, things exploding, and musical numbers were where he shone! Albrecht would have to go back and warn Dave what was coming.

CHAPTER 14

Albrecht ran through the night to warn Dave. By the time he reached the castle it was nearly dawn, and he still had to sneak his way into the party to find Dave. Luckily, Albrecht always has a plan.

Inside the great hall everyone was at the National Dave Day party. Knights were filling themselves with snacks all over again, peasants were eating both kinds of Rat-On-A-Stick, Mildred was there with her girls with moustashes and, oh yes, all the ambassadors. Albrecht could just about see Dave through the mass. He elbowed party guests out the way and even had to butt one or two to reach the King.

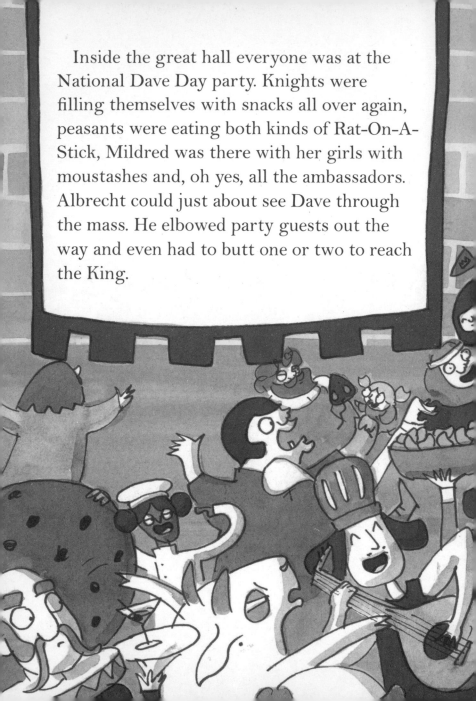

No time! This is an emergency!

I'm far too busy with this party for...

No Dave! This is important.

Oh yes! Albrecht? Sandwich?

LISTEN!

So you don't want a sandwich?

 ingdom being invaded?

 rmy at your gates?

 ot sure what to do?

 et your knights to repel the invaders.

OR

Have your peasants fight them off.

OR

Ask your ambassador friends to lend a hand.

CHAPTER 15

While Dave was busy reading *Royalty for Beginners,* the sun had risen and Belinda was at the gates.

'OK, don't panic!' said Dave. 'As King I shall sort this out. Knights! Go and defend the castle!'

But the knights weren't about to help.

'Right, not a problem. Peasants, fight off those intruders!'

But the peasants wouldn't help either.

'You lot might not be loyal to the crown, but I know my ambassador friends will come to my aid.'

What? Who? Me?

I just remembered I have a dentist appointment.

I think we might have outstayed our welcome.

Oh look at the time. I must be going.

But the ambassadors were not very good friends.

Dave didn't take this well.

OFF WITH THEIR HEADS!

CHAPTER 16

It occurred to Albrecht that Dave wasn't coping well with this crisis. He would have to step in.

As soon as Dave stopped shouting, the party guests took the opportunity to flee the great hall and presumably the soon-to-be invaded castle.

Albrecht pushed through the crowds and caught Dave by the hand. 'Come Dave, there is a place in this castle that I think you should see.'

Albrecht led Dave through deserted corridors and up the spiral staircases. All the while Dave could hear the sound of Belinda's army getting ready outside. Eventually, Albrecht pushed open a very old wooden door and they entered the gallery full of paintings.

'Dave, these are the portraits of all the kings and queens that have ever ruled this kingdom,' said Albrecht. 'I have learnt a lot about them while we've been staying here and I think you should hear what people say about them now.'

Albrecht started walking off down the corridor with his hooves clasped behind his back and began to talk about the paintings. Dave totted along behind him.

This is King
Goosegerry I, who
spent all the money
on fancy cats.

And King Goosegerry
II, is known as the
worse king because he
was rumoured to spend
his free time kicking
the fancy cats. Also, he
ate some of them.

King Affnong IV,
spent all his time
looking at pretty
clouds as the
kingdom burned.

Queen Glendina III,
thought she was so
mighty that even the
largest boulder would
not squash her.

Queen Fiona V, built
the most fabulous
palace the world had
ever seen, but used
all the stone so the
peasants had to sleep in
boxes.

Queen Davina I,
beheaded all the
knights because
she didn't like their
hairstyles.

King Fargo I, didn't like being king much, so gave the job to a frog. The frog was a terrible diplomat and plunged the kingdom to a 100 year war.

The current king is mainly known for his many divorces but Rubella is trying to rebrand him as an environmentally friendly king.

'Oh gosh, I know what they're going to say about me!' said Dave as he plonked himself down on the floor of the gallery. 'They'll call me terrible temporary King Dave who was so busy with pool parties that he handed the kingdom to a Potato lady! Not just that, I have been a really rubbish friend. I'm sorry, Albrecht. It's just that all this being King got a bit on top of me . . . but there's no excuse really.'

Dave started to get very snuffly. 'I don't want to do this anymore, Albrecht! It's too difficult. Can you be King instead? Here, take the crown.'

Dave took the crown off and tried to hand it over to Albrecht, but he backed away.

'Dave, I cannot be the king. I'm already King of the Seagulls, remember? Also, you can't just give up because you made some mistakes. The thing about being a leader is that when you fail you get back on that goat and try again.'

Dave looked unconvinced.

Albrecht sat down next to Dave, pulled a slightly smelly hanky from somewhere in his fur and

— But. Albrecht, I'm not a good King!

gave it to him. Dave blew his noble nose loudly.

'Plan for a siege. OK let's do that,' said Dave.'
'I'll have a look in the book.'

o you're under Siege

ather your huge army.

ake a rousing speech to inspire your troops.

epel the invaders by any means.

'Oh look!' said Dave 'There's even a page about what to do in my situation.'

If you don't have any knights and the peasants won't help then turn to page 100.

You are now under siege.

You have lost your knights and angered your peasants.

You have done a terrible job of

being King and now your Kingdom will be taken and you will probably die.

CHAPTER 17

'Well that's not very encouraging,' said Dave.

'We do not have to do this by the book, Dave!' said Albrecht. 'We can raise our own army.'

Dave and Albrecht ran back into the great hall looking for party guests to enlist in their army. Almost everyone had decided the party was probably over and that there was a bit of an invasion problem in this castle so maybe it was time to leave.

Despite this, a few brave souls had stayed behind to help out, and they were ready to fight! Or ready to finish the leftover party food, one or the other.

No one appreciates our food like King Dave!

Dave was delighted. 'Right troops, you are now all that stands between our freedom and a life of potato slavery! The book can't help us now, so I'm relying on your bravery. Oh gosh, never has a king been so proud.' Dave started to dab his eyes.

'I don't know why he's crying,' said Miranda to Albrecht. 'If I wasn't here this army would be rubbish.'

Dave assembled his forces on the battlement

Myself and my girls will defend the kingdom.

I don't have anything better to do.

and leaned over the edge to get a look at the invaders. That is when he came face-to-face with Queen Belinda of Potatoland.

No thank you. It would be much nicer if you just went home!

'I can't do that! Proper royals don't shy away from battles,' Belinda shouted up to Dave. 'This means WAR! I'll give you five minutes to use the toilet or tie your shoes or whatever but then we're going to attack!'

'That's not a very nice thing to do but if you insist!' Dave shouted back.

Dave stood up and looked at his troops. Seeing Belinda's huge army had given him that sicky feeling in his stomach. Dave knew he had to be brave though so that his troops would be brave too, so he concentrated really hard on stopping his hands from shaking.

'This seems as good a moment as any to make a rousing speech, Your Majesty,' said Albrecht.

'Oh OK,' said Dave straightening his crown. Now was his moment to act brave. 'Hi everyone. Thank you for coming today to this war at such short notice.'

'HUZZAH!' cheered the troops.

'Did someone say something?' said Miranda.

I may have the body of a green and short dragon but I have the stomach of a temporary King who's kingdom-sitting for a week! I will do everything I can to defend this castle and your freedom!

'Huzzah?' the troops cheered again.

'When will there be cream?' said Miranda.

Dave puffed up. 'I may not have been the best King up until now, and I haven't been very nice to my subjects or my friends. What I have learned from this is that we need help from the people around us. I know that if we all work together we shall prevail! So, remember everyone, try your best, and it's not the winning but the taking part that counts.'

Albrecht coughed.

'Oh, actually, in this case winning is pretty important because otherwise we'll be overrun by potatoes but, you know, good luck and thanks for listening.'

'Erm, long live the King?' cheered the troops.

And so they all went to use the toilet in preparation for Belinda's attack.

Plan your defences

Lock the back door.

Fire lots of arrows!

CHAPTER 18

Belinda's attacks were relentless.

Flags are good.

Everyone loves boiling oil!

Don't forget to close the gate!

First came the mashed potato.

But Dave had the chefs take care of that.

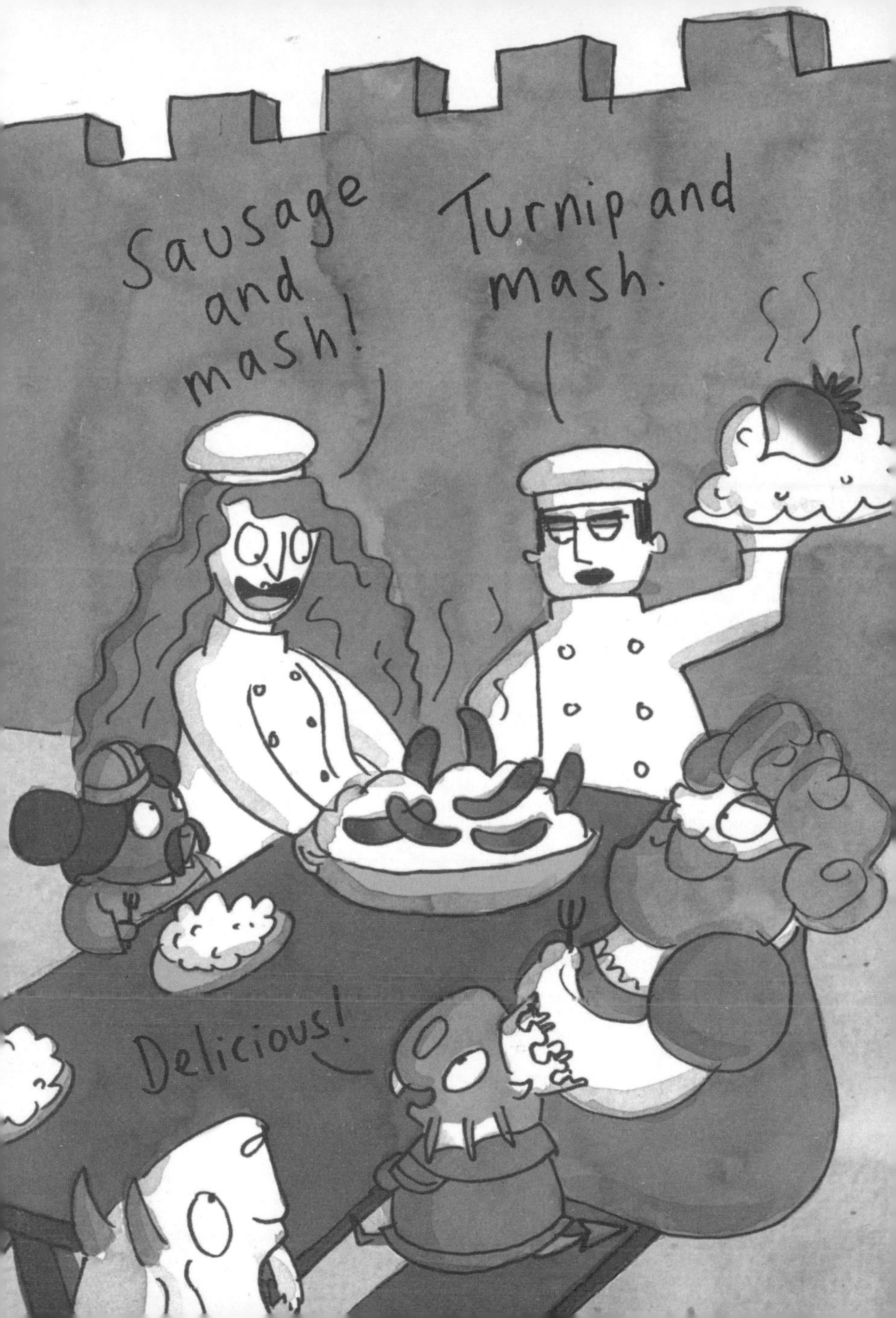
Sausage and mash!
Turnip and mash.
Delicious!

Then they tried tunnelling under the walls.

But as soon as Dave noticed he had Miranda deal with that.

Belinda even tried saying mean things to hurt their feelings.

You're green and you stink! You may as well give up now.

If you were a potato, you'd be a STUPID potato!

But it turned out Bearded Lady and her girls with moustaches were much better at it.

I'd be scared if you were as bad as you smell!

Come on. I'm not as stupid as you look.

Go home, Belinda! You're depriving a village somewhere of its idiot.

Overall, Dave thought the siege was going rather better than expected.

The next day though Dave noticed there was a problem. Water was running low.

Everyone was getting very thirsty.

'I should never have built that pool!' thought Dave. 'That water is undrinkable now; Boil Man went in there!'

Dave had a difficult decision to make.

Either he could stay in the besieged castle and keep his crown but his troops would suffer . . .

... or he could surrender his crown to Belinda, and she would ravish the kingdom with potatoes.

Things were not looking good, so Dave was preparing for the worst. He and Albrecht had gone to the King's chambers to hide the valuables. Belinda might get the kingdom but she'd never get Rubella's stamp collection. As they worked Dave and Albrecht talked the problem over.

'That is a hard decision for anyone to make,' said Albrecht. 'But that is what being king is all about. You must do what you think is best and I shall support you whatever.'

Dave sighed and hid a few gold goblets and more stamps under the floorboards. 'I've decided. I think being king means that sometimes you have to give it all up for your subjects.'

'So it's not having huge portraits painted of yourself?' said Albrecht with a raised eyebrow.

'On reflection, no, probably not. Though the artist did do a good job of my nose. But anyway, I'm going to hand over the crown and surrender. I can't let my troops suffer.' Dave picked up the Special Occasion Crown and tried to fit it under the bed.

'That is a selfless decision, mein Dave, but this

means the kingdom is doomed. The King and Princess Rubella will be a tad miffed when they get back from the conference. Plus we can't let Belinda get away with this. If I were in charge, even if she took my kingdom, I would take her kingdom right back!'

Dave stopped and stared at the big crown in his hands. 'Do you know, I think you might have a point there, Albrecht.' Dave seemed deep in thought. 'I wouldn't worry yet, Albrecht. I might have a plan.'

CHAPTER 19

Belinda snatched the message and began to read. 'It's from King Dave. He says he going to come out and surrender. Victory is ours!'

Belinda was secretly rather impressed by King Dave. He'd been much harder to defeat than expected, especially for a temporary king who'd only been in the job for a few days. And this didn't come a moment too soon; they were almost out of potatoes. Still, she'd better get ready for Dave to come out. After all, it's not every day you conquer a kingdom.

Surrounded by her generals and finest troops, Belinda watched as Dave emerged from the castle.

CREEAK

Your Majesty, I surrender.

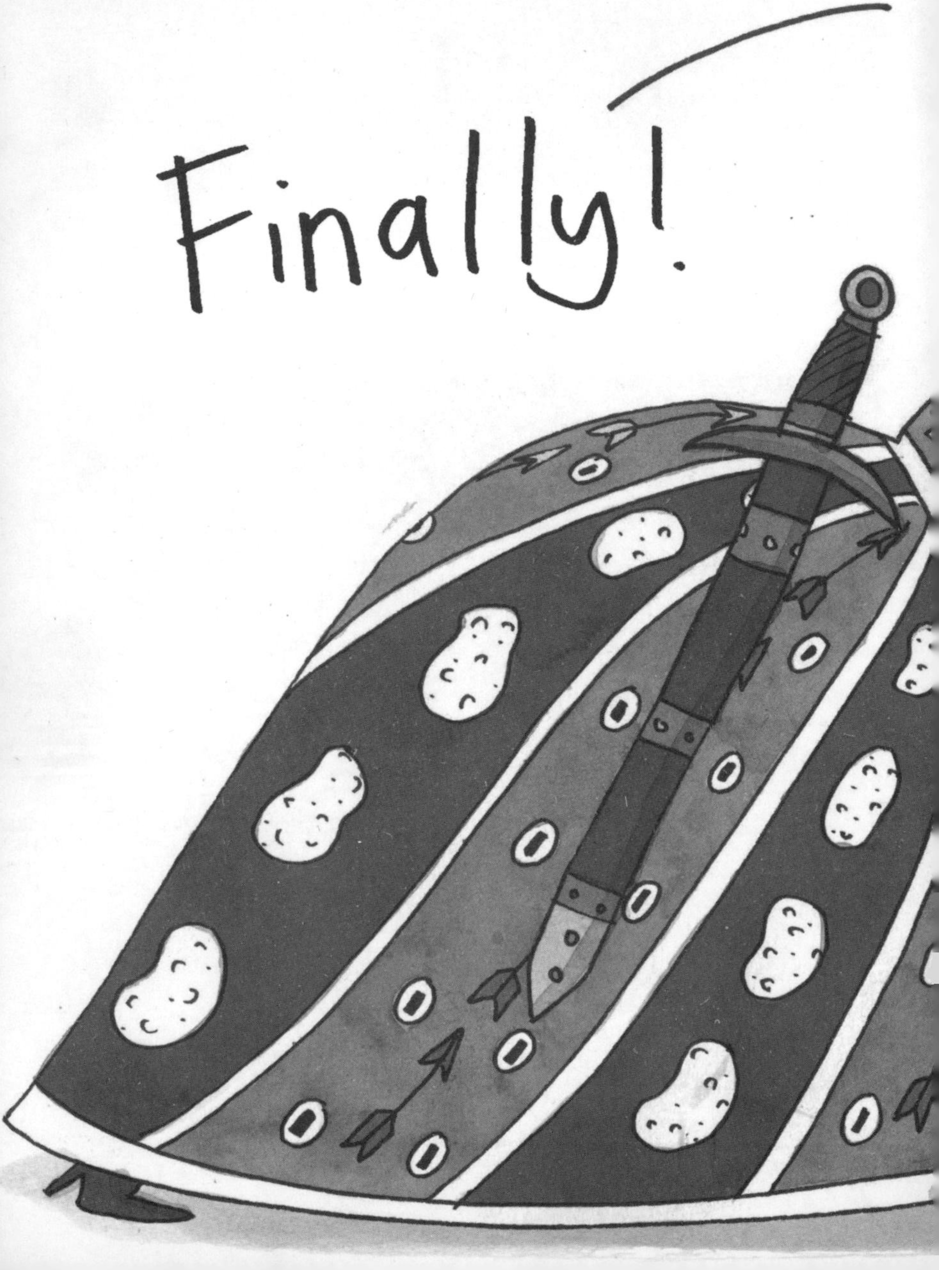
Finally!

NOW THE
KINGDOM
IS MINE!

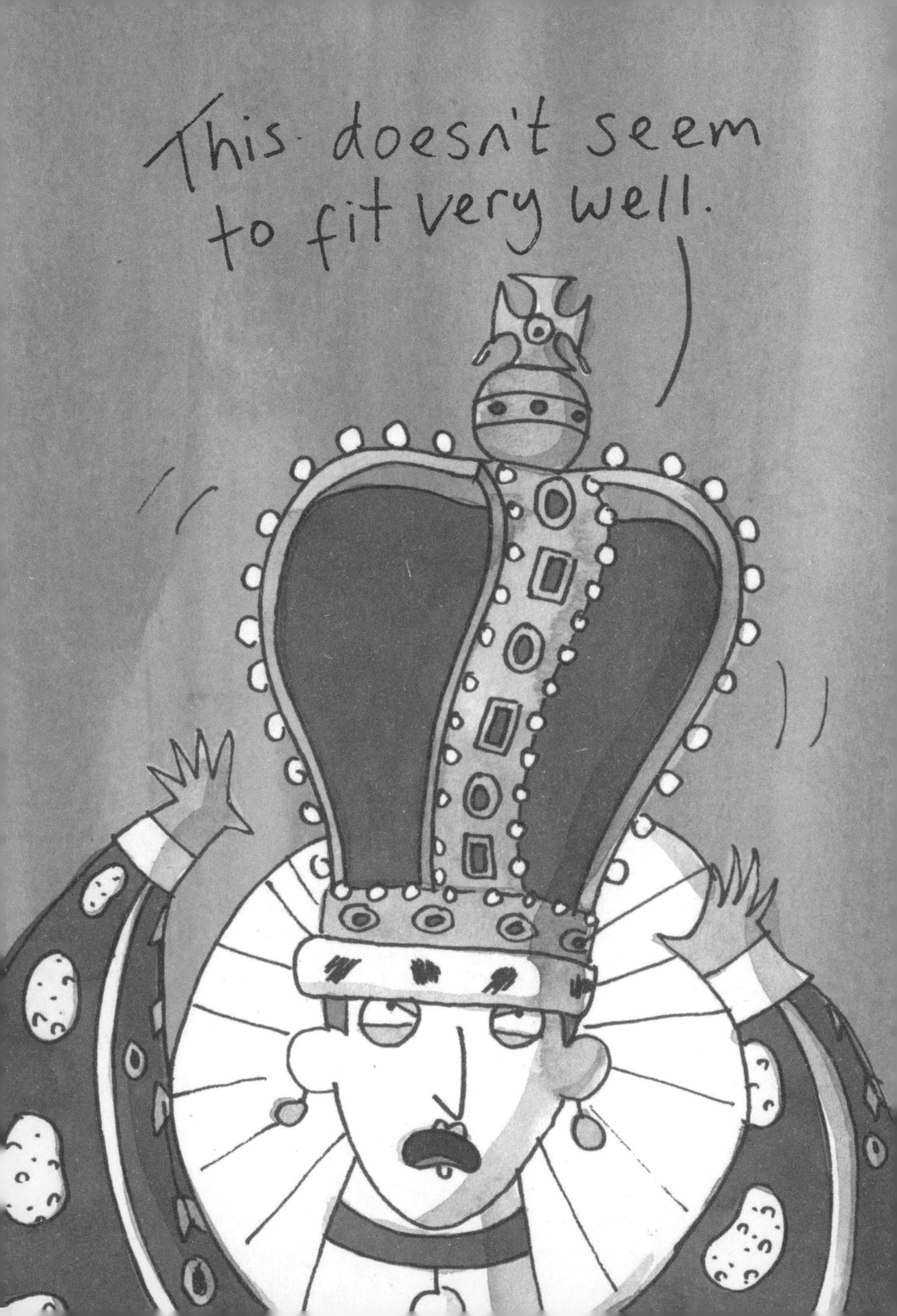
This doesn't seem to fit very well.

CHAPTER 20

This was perhaps not the glorious beginning of
her reign that Belinda had expected.

What's she saying?
I don't Know!
Your Majesty! What are your orders?
MURPH!
MURPH!
MUR!
Aha!

It was time for Dave to address a new set of subjects. He coughed and put on his most kingly voice.

'People of Potatoland! As you know, the rules are that whoever wears the crown is the King. Now that I wear the Potatoland crown, Belinda is no longer your Queen. Instead I am your King, Dave!'

The Potatoland troops gasped and dropped to their knees in front of their new king. Dave heard someone in the crowd whisper 'them's the rules'. Inside, Dave was rather shocked that this was actually working, but he knew that outside he had to appear his most regal.

'As your king I order you all to stop this siege at once. It's very rude. Then you must go back to Potatoland and try to be much nicer to people in future. Also, maybe try eating some other vegetables, like peas; I'm worried you don't have a very balanced diet.'

The army started to look up at Dave with puzzled expressions.

'Um, I mean, you must serve your king and show loyalty to me! Do as you're told, um, please!'

The soldiers looked around at each other, shrugged, and started to pack up and wander off. Belinda was left behind on the battlefield, wandering around with her shouting muffled by the Special Occasion Crown over her head. Dave had done it! He'd saved the kingdom, defeated Belinda, and was even still a king. Victory to Dave!

CHAPTER 21

The next morning when the King and Princess Rubella returned to the castle, they were not impressed with what they found.

'First the keynote speaker doesn't turn up at

our conference, and now look at the state of the castle,' said the King. 'Look, they didn't even remember to put the bins out!'

'I've got to admit, I'm not too unhappy about the swimming pool in the courtyard,' said Rubella.

'I wouldn't trust that pool. The colour of the water suggests that Boil Man has been in there,' said the King.

Rubella strode over to the wall and pulled down a poster. 'And what on earth is National Dave Day?'

'I'm thirsty,' said the King. 'Butler, please bring me . . . hang on, where is the butler? And where's the other staff?'

'More to the point, where are Dave and Albrecht?' said Rubella. 'They've got some explaining to do.'

Leaving their bags in the hall, Rubella and the King marched towards the doors to the great hall.

'And now they're throwing an unofficial party! Right, that's it!' Rubella stormed towards Dave who was passing out finger sandwiches to his victorious troops.

'Dave! What on earth is going on here?!' said Rubella.

'Well, I've made some sandwiches for everyone because they've worked really hard. Would you like one? They're cucumber.'

'That's not what I mean! The castle is a state, there's potato everywhere for reasons I do not understand, and the chefs are doing the conga instead of cooking! I have never seen a more irresponsible, destructive, or green king in my life! Well, apart from maybe Dad in the great paint explosion of 1524.'

Taken aback, Dave was about to try and explain when Albrecht stepped in front of him.

'Halt princess! You do not know what happened here. King Dave has just fought off an invasion from a potato power-mad queen without a single knight, and now you're shouting at him like a big DUMMKOPF!'

Dave watched Rubella go very pink and even more furious at Albrecht's words and decided he'd better step in.

'What Albrecht means to say,' said Dave pushing past Albrecht, 'is that we had a bit of bother with a little invasion . . .'

Rubella and the King worked their way through the finger sandwiches as Dave explained about Queen Belinda, the siege, and how they finally prevailed.

'So you see that Potatoland ambassador was there just to mislead me and make sure that I and all the other ambassadors got carried away with all the parties. Belinda never intended to go to that conference; it was all to get you out of the way,' said Dave, offering them the last of the sandwiches.

'Well, that would explain why Belinda never turned up to the conference,' said the King. 'King of Potatoland! Well I never! Good show old chap! What did you do with Belinda?'

'Miranda has been keeping an eye on her in the kitchens,' said Albrecht.

Let's get this back to the King.

'Miranda mentioned that you should probably have this back.' Dave took the Special Occasion Crown off the statue next to him and gave it back to the King who immediately plonked it on his own, rather large, head.

'Oh yes, wouldn't want to lose that!' said the King. 'And I'd say a victory party even counts as a special occasion. Golly, Miranda! That terrifying specimen has been working here for ages. Maybe it's time I gave her a promotion. What do you think, Dave my boy?'

'I think something like Official Guardian of the Cream would please her,' said Dave.

'Then that's what she shall be!' said the King. 'So Dave, you'd say kingdom-sitting went rather well then, eh?'

'Oh yes, everything was just fine the whole time . . .' Then Dave caught Albrecht's eye. 'Well, actually I think I got a little carried away.'

So Dave explained about the parties, the ambassadors, the swimming pool, and why he thought there shouldn't be another National Dave Day next year.

'Oh Dave, us royals always get a little carried

away with ourselves at some point! You should have seen all the statues I had made of myself as a young man! All my wives hated them.'

'They would have been a lot better if you had been wearing clothes in any of them!' said Rubella. 'Anyway, the important thing Dave, is that you overcame all the obstacles and saved our kingdom. Good job.'

'He couldn't have done it without me,' said Albrecht smugly.

'What are you going to do now as the King of Potatoland?' said the King. 'As king you could banish Belinda and rule your own kingdom.'

Dave thought about this. The crowns, the parties, the power and the outfits! And this time with all his experience of being a king he would be so much more glorious! Albrecht gave him a sidelong look.

'Frankly, Your Majesty, if I can't share the job with Albrecht I don't think it's for me. I think I'll just keep being your hero consultant and work on my baking. I've done more than enough kinging for now.'

'In that case what are we going to do about

Belinda? If you return the crown to her, there's nothing to stop her from returning to Potatoland, raising another army and invading again.'

Dave thought for a moment. 'Albrecht showed me a very useful trick for showing royals the error of their ways. Let me take care of it.'

There, there. The picture gallery has this effect on all of us.

They're going to call me the crazy potato lady! That's awful! I need to diversify!

AND THEY ALL LIVED HAPPILY EVER AFTER

Rat-On-A-Stick guy and Boil Man are still at odds over their snack sales. The King decreed that both were too delicious to ban. Now they keep to separate sides of town to avoid fist fights.

Mildred the Bearded Lady won this year's Castletown Open. She's now training for the Olympics.

To commemorate the 'Battle for Castletown' as it became known, the girls with moustaches sewed a fabulous tapestry.

The King did eventually meet Queen Belinda. She gave him a signed photo, but she refused to marry him. Rubella said you should never meet your heroes.

As a tribute to their temporary king, the castle chefs invented a new pudding called National Dave Dessert.

Miranda and Albrecht did go for that coffee, and there are rumours flying around Castletown saying that they've been dating for a while now. Dave thinks it's probably a love-hate relationship.

Dave hasn't ruled a kingdom since, but when the King isn't around Rubella sometimes lets him wear the Special Occasion Crown.

The King told Dave that, on reflection, he thinks Dave did a pretty top-hole job of being king, but he hadn't seen the huge portrait in his bedroom at that point.

DAVE!

CROWN COUPON

1 free starter crown per customer

10% OFF

CASTLE

EXTENSIONS

WE MAKE YOUR TINY
CASTLE COMPLETELY

MASSIVE!

TURRET SPECIALIST

Albrecht's German
for Dummköpfe

aufwachen – wake up

dumme – stupid

Dummkopf – fool, blockhead (singular)

Dummköpfe – fools, blockheads (plural)

Fräulein – Miss, young lady

Guten Tag – Good day

Herr – Mr

Ich kann sprechen – I can speak

ja – yes (pronounced yah)

kleiner Drache – little dragon

kleine Suppenwerfer – small soup thrower

Können Sie mich verstehen? – Can you understand me?

magisch – magical

mein – my

mein Dorfesser – my village eater

mein Hintern – my bottom

Mein Gott! Ich kann sprechen! – My God! I can talk!

mein Dave – my Dave

mein kleiner grüner (friend) – my little green (friend)

Rotzlöffel – snot-spoon

Sauerkraut – pickled cabbage

schnell – quickly

über – outstanding, utmost, extremely

Unterhose – underpants

wunderbar - wonderful

ELYS DOLAN

Elys is an author and illustrator currently living and working in Cambridge. She works predominantly with ink, newfangled digital witchcraft, and coloured pencils, of which she is the proud owner of 178 but can never seem to find a sharpener. When not doing pictures and making things up, Elys enjoys growing cacti, collecting pocket watches, and eating excessive amounts of fondant fancies.

Elys Dolan's first young fiction book *Knighthood for Beginners* was shortlisted for the Branford Boase Award; her hilarious picture books have been shortlisted for *The Roald Dahl Funny Prize, Waterstones Children's Book Prize,* and nominated for the *Kate Greenaway Medal.*

More from
Dave and Albrecht . . .

KNIGHTHOOD for BEGINNERS

'Full of splendid silliness' *The Guardian*

FROM THE
MOST BONKERS MIND OF
ELYS DOLAN

Dave dreams of being a brave, knightly knight—saving princesses, riding a majestic steed, and protecting the kingdom from all evil-doers. And when he finds a very special book, *Knighthood for Beginners*, his quest to become a knight begins!

Accompanied by his trusty steed, Albrecht, he duels with the strongest and bravest knights in the land. But his toughest test comes when he has to convince the court that being rather small, distinctly green, and, frankly, A DRAGON, is no barrier to knighthood.

WIZARDING
FOR
BEGINNERS
WIZARDING FOR BEGINNERS
'Dolan's surreal, outrageous humour gives her work perennial child-appeal.' The Guardian.
ELYS DOLAN

When Terrence the Terrible kidnaps the talking animals of Castletown there are only two brave heroes who can stop him. Dave the dragon knight, and his best friend, and trusty steed Albrecht the goat!

Together they plan to sneak into the Wizard Guild undercover, and teach that trickster Terrence a lesson. All with the help of very special book—
Wizarding for Beginners!

But nothing is straight forward, especially in the Wizard Guild, where they have some crazy rules:

- No running, except on Thursdays.
- No shoes on the carpet unless it's a full moon.
- Shortest wizard wears the Tea Time Hat!

And worst of all . . .
Absolutely NO girls allowed!

More from Elys Dolan

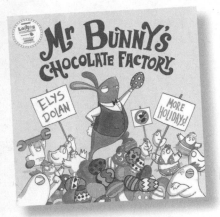